D1536237

EDGE
BOOKS™

DRAWING COOL STUFF

HOW TO DRAW

FEROCIOUS
ANIMALS

by Aaron Sautter

illustrated by Steve Erwin
and Charles Barnett III

Capstone
press®

Mankato, Minnesota

Edge Books are published by Capstone Press,
151 Good Counsel Drive, P.O. Box 669, Mankato, Minnesota 56002.
www.capstonepress.com

Library of Congress Cataloging-in-Publication Data
Sautter, Aaron.
    How to draw ferocious animals / by Aaron Sautter; illustrated by Steve Erwin
and Charles Barnett III.
    p. cm. — (Edge books. Drawing cool stuff)
    Includes bibliographical references and index.
    Summary: "Lively text and fun illustrations describe how to draw ferocious
animals" — Provided by publisher.
    ISBN–13: 978-1-4296-1299-9 (hardcover)
    ISBN–10: 1-4296-1299-1 (hardcover)
    1. Animals in art — Juvenile literature. 2. Wildlife art — Juvenile literature.
3. Drawing — Technique — Juvenile literature. I. Erwin, Steve. II. Barnett III,
Charles. III. Title. IV. Series.
NC780.S228 2008
743.6 — dc22   2007025104

Credits
Jason Knudson, set designer; Patrick D. Dentinger, book designer

1 2 3 4 5 6 13 12 11 10 09 08

TABLE OF CONTENTS

Welcome!

You probably picked this book because you think big, wild animals are cool. Or you picked it because you like to draw. Whatever the reason, get ready to dive into the world of ferocious animals!

Our world is filled with fearsome animals. Vicious reptiles, meat-eating cats, and big bears are just a few of the predators that live on our planet. Whether you like savage sharks or huge charging elephants, one thing is certain — you don't want them coming after you!

This book is just a starting point. Once you've learned how to draw the different animals in this book, you can start drawing your own. Let your imagination run wild, and see what sorts of fierce animals you can create!

To get started, you'll need some supplies:

1. First you'll need drawing paper. Any type of blank, unlined paper will do.

2. Pencils are the easiest to use for your drawing projects. Make sure you have plenty of them.

3. You have to keep your pencils sharp to make clean lines. Keep a pencil sharpener close by. You'll use it a lot.

4. As you practice drawing, you'll need a good eraser. Pencil erasers wear out very fast. Get a rubber or kneaded eraser. You'll be glad you did.

5. When your drawing is finished, you can trace over it with a black ink pen or thin felt-tip marker. The dark lines will really make your work stand out.

6. If you decide to color your drawings, colored pencils and markers usually work best. You can also use colored pencils to shade your drawings and make them more lifelike.

GREAT WHITE SHARK

Great white sharks are ferocious predators. They grow to about 16 feet long. Their mouths often have as many as 3,000 sharp, jagged teeth. You don't want to come face-to-face with one of these huge "wolves of the sea!"

After drawing this shark, try drawing a bunch more in a feeding frenzy!

STEP 1

STEP 2

STEP 3

STEP 4

FINAL!

7

HIPPOPOTAMUS

Although a hippopotamus looks friendly, it's best to keep your distance. These massive 4,000-pound mammals can be very aggressive. And they can run faster than people for short distances. If you see one of these in the wild, be ready to quickly climb a tree!

When you're done drawing this beast, try showing a bunch of them grazing on the African plain.

STEP 1

STEP 2

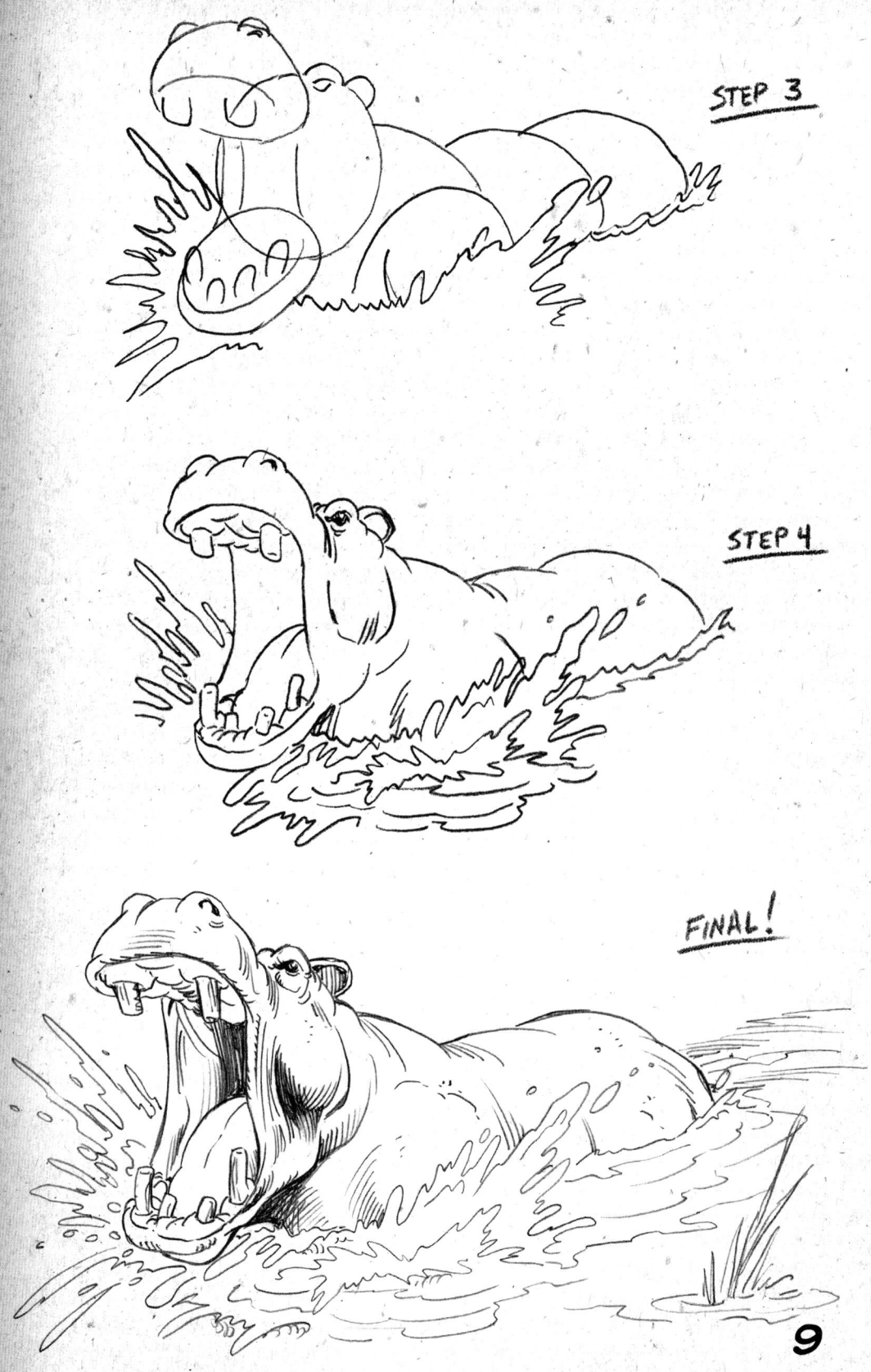

STEP 3

STEP 4

FINAL!

9

MOUNTAIN LION

If you go on a vacation to the Rocky Mountains, keep an eye out for hungry mountain lions. Also known as cougars, these big cats can weigh as much as 160 pounds. Mountain lions hardly ever attack people. But if you see one, be sure to keep your distance!

After drawing this big cat, try it again as it hunts for a tasty rabbit.

STEP 1

STEP 2

10

STEP 3

STEP 4

FINAL!

11

GRIZZLY BEAR

Hiking in Alaska can be a lot of fun — unless you meet an angry grizzly bear! These big bears weigh as much as 1,500 pounds. They can also run up to 35 miles per hour. Don't try to run away. Instead, drop to the ground and play dead. It might be your only defense.

After practicing this bear, try showing him fishing for some Alaskan salmon!

STEP 1

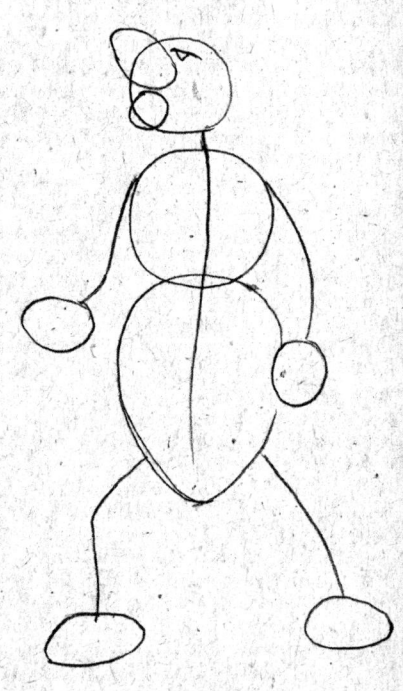

STEP 2

STEP 3

STEP 4

FINAL!

13

KOMODO DRAGON

At about 10 feet long and 350 pounds, Komodo dragons are the biggest lizards in the world. Their saliva is packed with deadly bacteria. Just one bite can infect and kill prey in just a few days. If you're ever in Indonesia, keep an eye out for these deadly reptiles!

After drawing this big lizard, try showing him swallowing his prey whole!

STEP 1

STEP 2

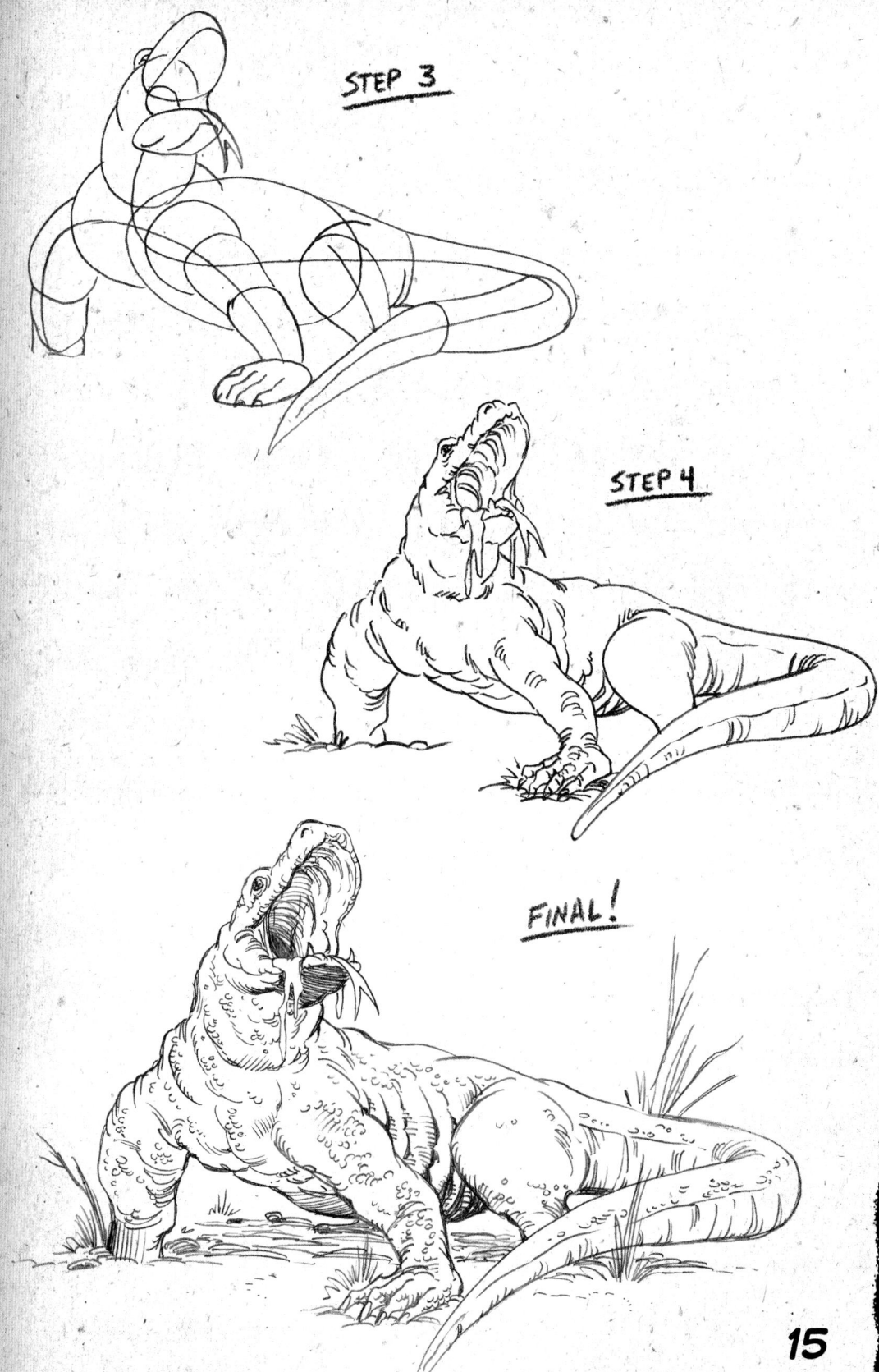

STEP 3

STEP 4

FINAL!

15

TIMBER WOLF

Wolves are the ancestors of dogs, but they're not man's best friend. They travel and hunt in packs, so if you see one, there are probably more wolves nearby. There is little to fear, though, because wolves rarely attack people. Just stay back, and they will leave you alone.

After drawing this wolf, try drawing a pack of them hunting an elk or moose!

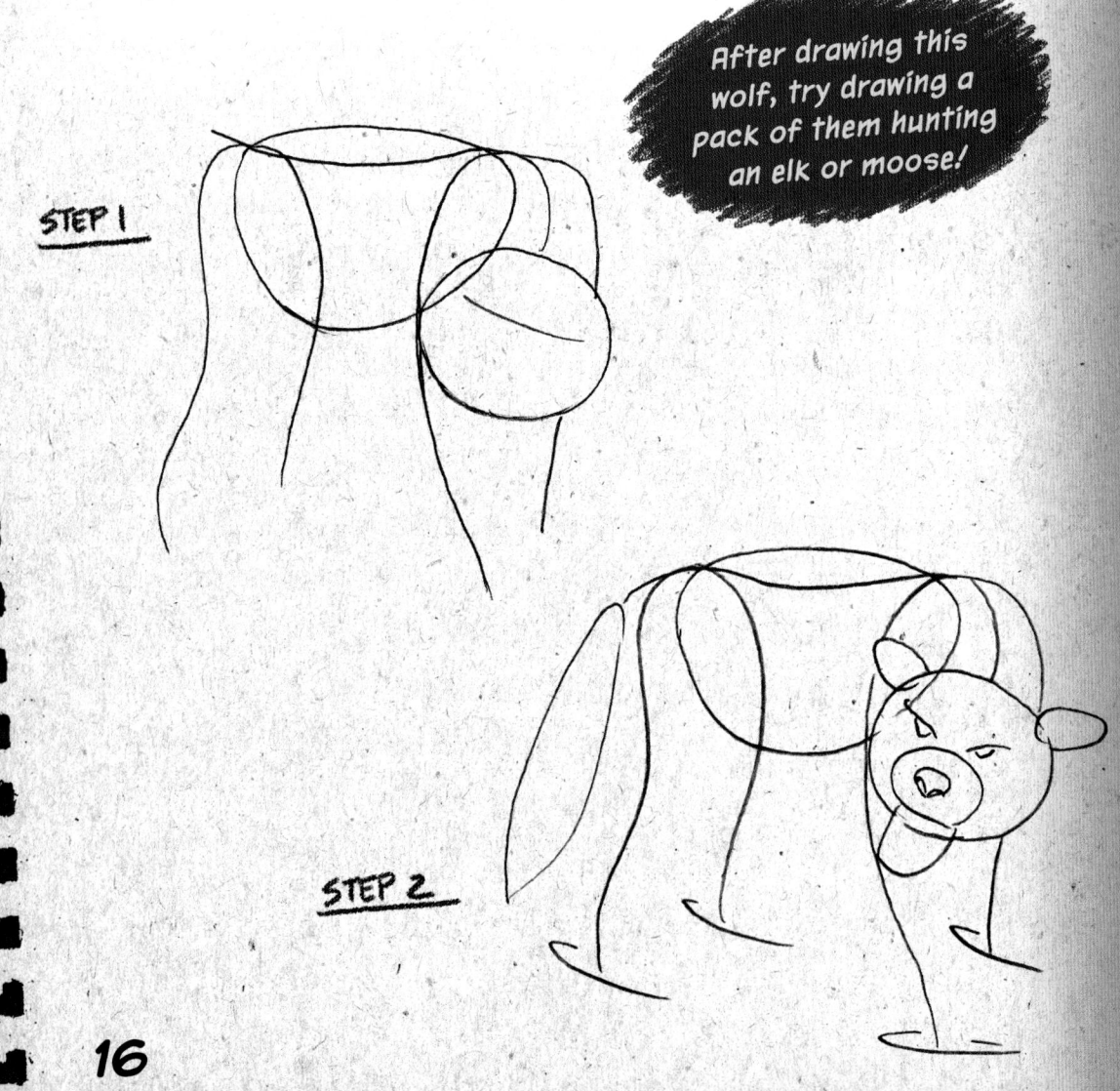

STEP I

STEP 2

STEP 3

STEP 4

FINAL!

BENGAL TIGER

Bengal tigers live mostly in India and Bangladesh. These big cats usually weigh about 500 pounds and are fierce predators. Their orange fur and black stripes help them hide in tall grass when hunting prey. They'll eat almost anything — even elephants!

After drawing this tiger, try showing it chasing down a water buffalo!

STEP 1

STEP 2

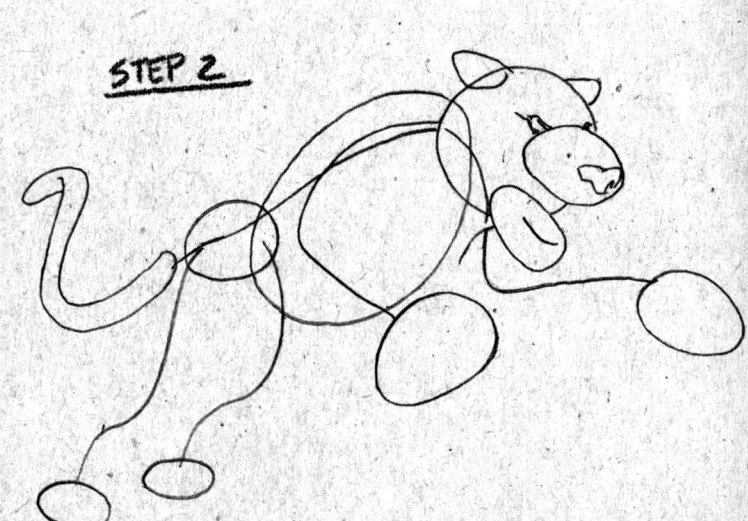

STEP 3

STEP 4

FINAL!

19

SILVERBACK GORILLA

Gorillas are the largest primates on earth. They stand up to 6 feet tall and weigh up to 500 pounds. Although gorillas are normally very gentle, you don't want a male silverback angry with you!

After drawing this ape, try showing a group of them resting in the jungle!

STEP 1

STEP 2

STEP 3

STEP 4

FINAL!

21

AFRICAN ELEPHANT

The African elephant is the largest land animal on Earth. These giant mammals can stand up to 12 feet tall and weigh as much as 22,000 pounds. If you see one of these charging at you, there's only one thing you can do — run!

Try showing this elephant grabbing some leaves from a tree with its trunk!

STEP 1

STEP 2

STEP 3

STEP 4

FINAL!

23

SALTWATER CROCODILE

Saltwater crocodiles are the largest reptiles living in the world today. These huge beasts can grow up to 23 feet long and weigh more than 3,300 pounds. Keep away from this monster, or it might think you'd make a tasty snack!

After drawing this big beast, try showing it lunging out of the water to grab its prey.

STEP 1

STEP 2

STEP 3

STEP 4

FINAL!

25

BATTLE UNDER THE SEA!

Giant squid are one of the sperm whale's main sources of food. Scientists think the whales and squid often have huge battles near the bottom of the sea. Many whales have been found with sucker-shaped scars covering their skin. If you could see one of these epic fights, it would be an amazing sight!

After mastering this battle, try drawing a grizzly bear fighting off a cougar or wolf!

STEP I

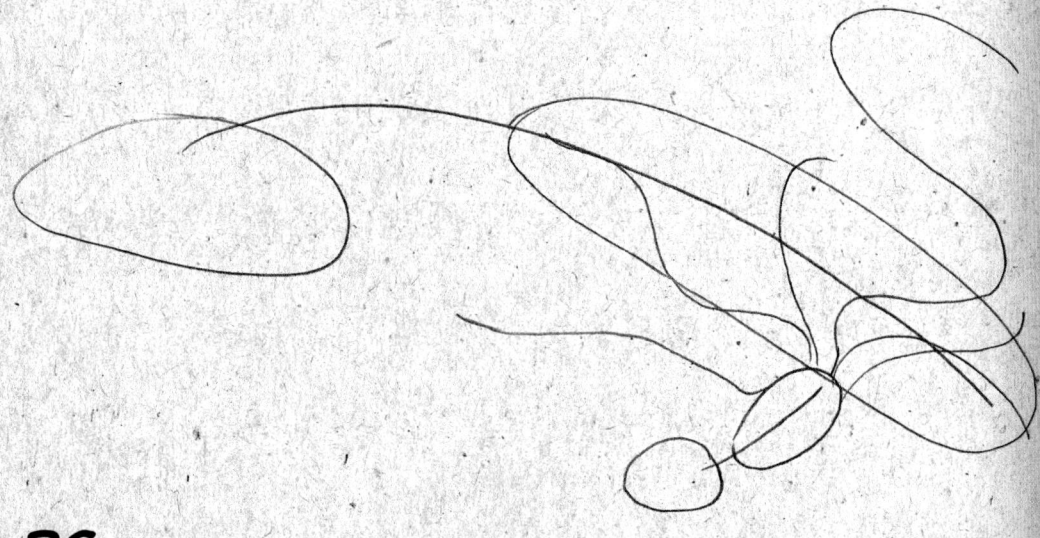

STEP 2

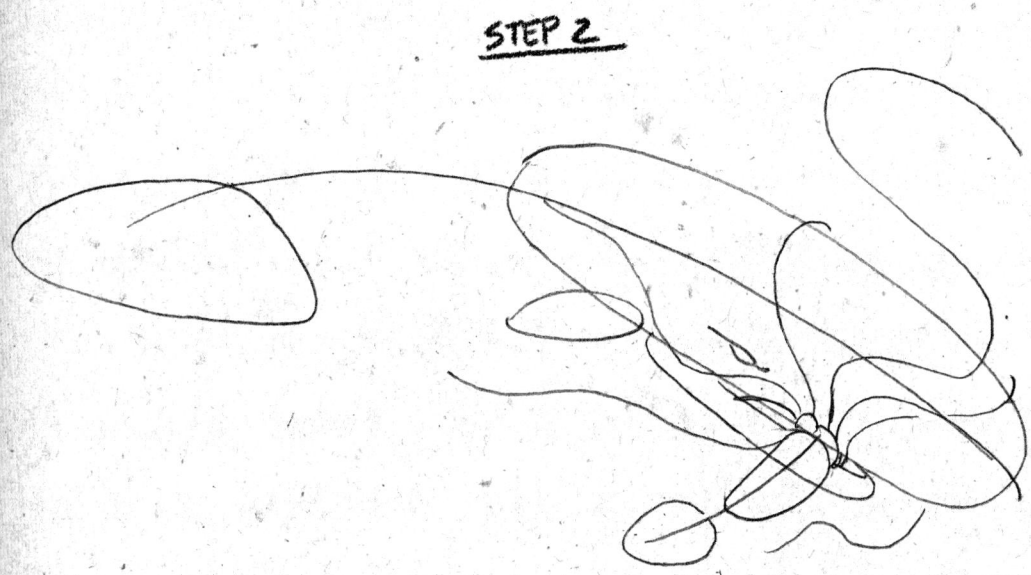

STEP 3

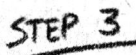

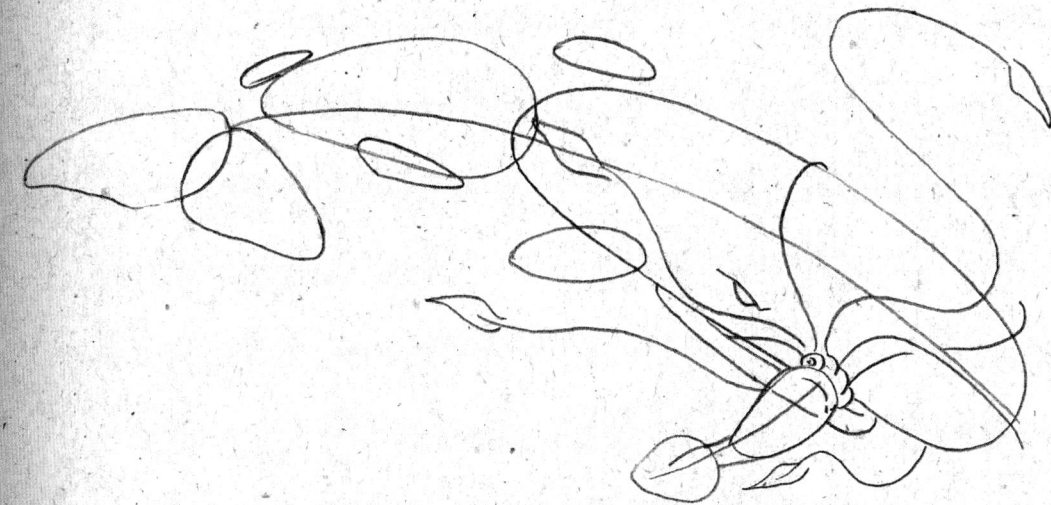

TO FINISH THIS DRAWING,
TURN TO THE NEXT PAGE!

STEP 4

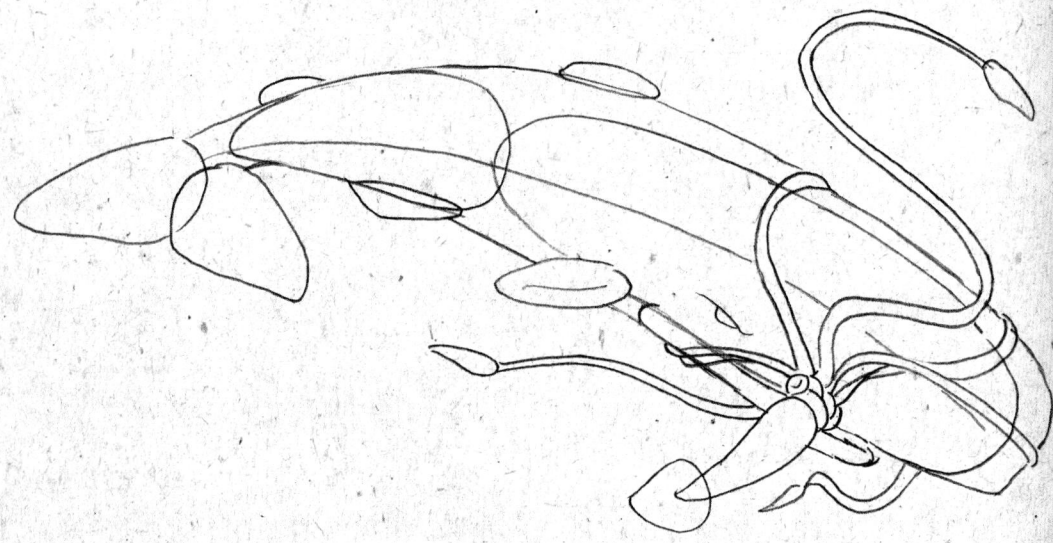

STEP 5

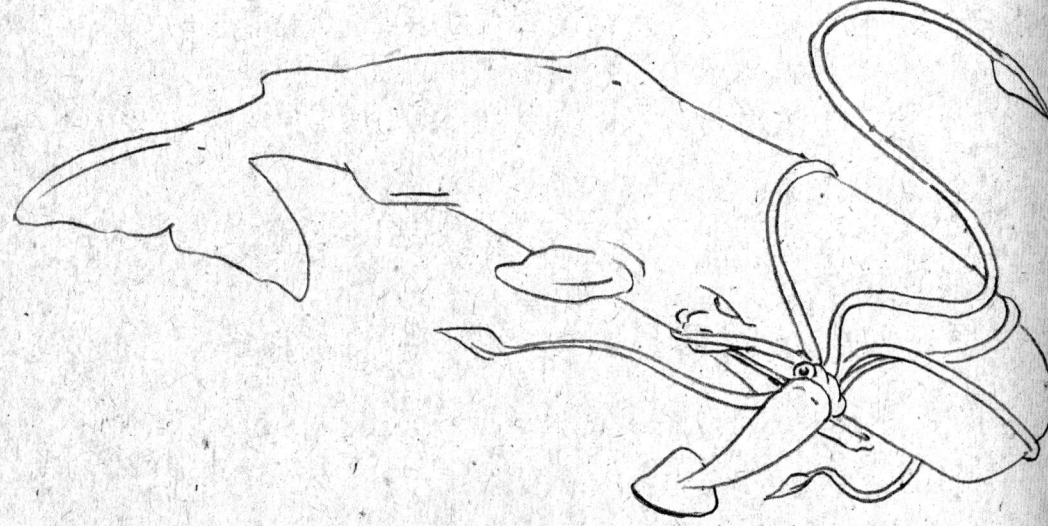

STEP 6

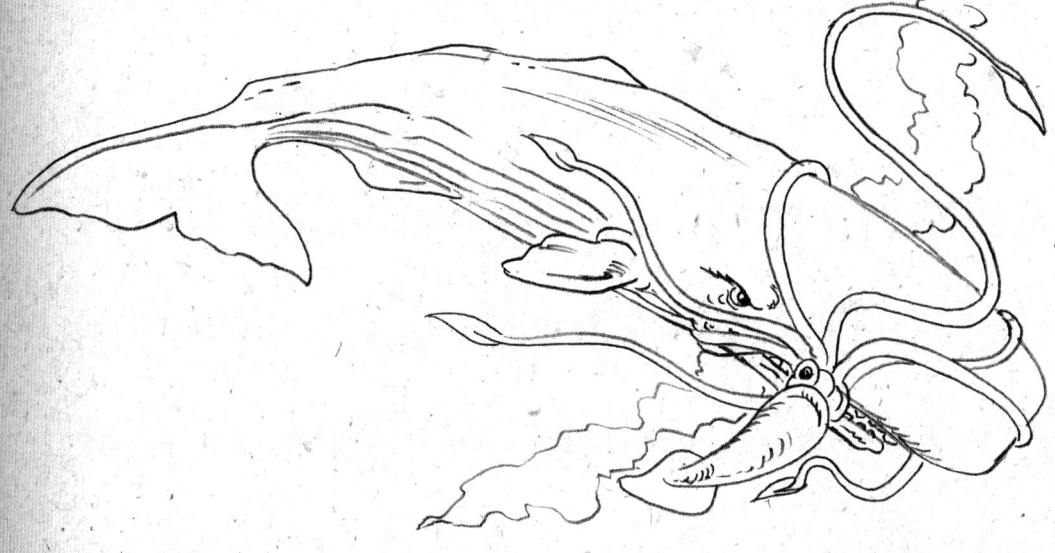

FINAL!

29

GLOSSARY

bacteria (bak-TEER-ee-uh) — very small organisms; some bacteria cause disease.

epic (EP-ik) — very large or impressive in size

mammal (MAM-uhl) — a warm-blooded animal that breathes air; female mammals feed milk to their young.

predator (PRED-uh-tur) — an animal that hunts and eats other animals

prey (PRAY) — an animal that is hunted and eaten by another animal

primate (PRYE-mate) — any animal in the group of mammals that includes humans, apes, and monkeys; primates use their fingers and thumbs to hold objects.

reptile (REP-tile) — a cold-blooded animal that breathes air and has a backbone; most reptiles lay eggs and have scaly skin.

READ MORE

Barr, Steve. *1-2-3 Draw Cartoon Wildlife: A Step-by-Step Guide.* 1-2-3 Draw. Columbus, N.C.: Peel Productions, 2003.

Hart, Christopher. *Kids Draw Animals.* Kids Draw. New York: Watson-Guptill, 2003.

Mack, Lorrie. *I Can Draw Animals.* I Can Draw. New York: DK, 2006.

INTERNET SITES

FactHound offers a safe, fun way to find Internet sites related to this book. All of the sites on FactHound have been researched by our staff.

Here's how:
1. Visit *www.facthound.com*
2. Choose your grade level.
3. Type in this book ID **1429612991** for age-appropriate sites. You may also browse subjects by clicking on letters, or by clicking on pictures and words.
4. Click on the **Fetch It** button.

FactHound will fetch the best sites for you!

INDEX